SPLINTER OF HOPE

JODY KAYE

Special Edition Paperback

First Print: January 2024

www.JodyKaye.com

Splinter of Hope
Shred of Decency
Sliver of Truth
Holding Onto Hope
Home Wrecker
Deep Gap
Bleeding Heart
Shattered Soul

I've already made

one decision that

shattered my heart...

For the Quinters, without whom this story
would have never been written.

Chapter One

Kimber

I stand in front of the mirror, fluffing my hands through my waist-length red hair one more time before applying sheer gloss to my lips.

At thirty-six years of age, I'm not sure why I need to look like I've stepped out of a magazine. Although, I accept that appearances matter. Today it's wholesome.

Last night?

Well, I manage Sweet Caroline's, the strip club across the street. So like the ladies who work for me, what I was—or rather wasn't wearing—is better left to the imagination.

I slip a silver cross around my neck as a reminder I have faith in myself to make it through the afternoon. Searching my jewelry drawer for a bracelet, I find the one I'm looking for without much effort. It's pounded metal with a wide cuff. The brilliant silver contrasts with the deep blue of my top. I slip it over the darkening contusion on my wrist, glad it covers the black and blue.

Trig will be beside himself when he sees the bruise.

It's not healthy of me to hide it from him, but in all fairness, now isn't the time to add to whatever he's worried about.

My phone dings on the dresser and my heart speeds up, pounding in my chest the way it does on the back of Trig's custom bike. I don't have to look to know the text is from him, and I can't explain the thrill it sends through me. The same freedom I find with the wind whipping through my hair on the open road is the way it feels loving this man.

Trig is constant and steady. He's borrowed a car and driven me where I need to go, any time I've needed to go there, for the past four years. It took a lot for me to decide to count on him. Now, lying in his arms at night, I'm not sure why.

I pick up an envelope on my nightstand, sliding out its contents to ensure I have the picture inside. I close my eyes. At first, this image is all I see. Then, like the residual spots of looking at something bright, the others I've given away over the past decade begin overlapping. Each one holds the memory of another girl with a very different story than the one I'd hoped for.

The picture goes back into the envelope to protect it. After it's safe in my purse, my pulse picks up again anticipating being with Trig. I open the door to my room, which is closest to the steps, and move the red velvet rope to the side. It's not much of a roadblock, more of a mental note to keep the barrier in place for the sake of others.

The first thing I see is Trig looking up at me from the last stair before the landing.

If it were any other day, I'd saunter over to him, swishing my ass back and forth. But today quick feet carry me those few steps to where I can feel the warmth of his body against mine.

On instinct, Trig reaches for my waist, setting his hands on my hips. I tilt my chin down and press my lips to his.

"You look gorgeous," he says. His steely eyes dance the same way his fingertips do against the gauzy fabric of my shirt.

"Thanks." I worry my lip.

"Big day." Still standing below me, Trig brushes my hair over my shoulder.

The third floor of the factory is off-limits to men. Carver designated the rooms up here for women only, so this is as far as any of the guys go. Part of it is respect for the ladies who live up here and an understanding that Carver is giving us a chance to change our lives. More than that, though is nobody would be as brash as to piss him off by breaking the long-standing rule. After all, the restored cotton mill is his building. We live here because Carver lets us.

None of us would ever sneak a man up here either. As a couple, we spend our private time in Trig's room on the floor just below. The guy's digs aren't as nice. I mean, it would be amazing if we had our own private bathrooms the way they do. But I wouldn't give up the space for a skinny shower stall since we have a sweet claw foot soaking tub up here.

I could use some of those relaxing bubbles about now.

"The biggest," I reply to Trig's big day comment with a huge sigh.

The corners of his kind eyes crinkle behind his dorky-but-oh-so-sexy horn rims. I run my fingers through his peppered gray hair.

As my hand comes forward, his lips catch the underside of my forearm. Trig trails light kisses to my palm.

I reach behind him, pulling his toque from his back pocket, and slipping it over his silver hair. "Your hat, My Love." The heat index in Eastern North Carolina could reach one-hundred, and he'd still put a knit cap on.

Trig gives me a lopsided grin. "It's good to be taken care of."

"It is," I agree, stepping beside him so we can walk hand-in-hand down to the parking lot.

At the next landing, right before we enter the lounge, Trig stops me. "I love you, Kimber."

"You told me last night. You showed me too." I waggle my brows, trying to lighten the mood.

Trig is my one long-term committed relationship. There won't be another like him, and I don't take one minute we're together for granted. Sometimes, you have to hold on to the splinter of hope that you've done your best for a person. Given them everything they needed… Accept when it's time to move on.

He pushes me against the stairwell wall. "Stop being kitschy or I'll ruin your lip gloss. I'm being serious."

"So am I. And I have more lip gloss in my bag. Ruin away."

Chapter Two

Trig

I've heard the dancers talking in the dressing room at Sweet Caroline's say some people kiss until they have to come up to catch their breath. Me? I choke on the air while waiting to kiss this woman. Letting Kimber slip from my bed this morning made me feel like I was drowning.

Kimber waltzed into my life four years ago. The moment I saw her, I decided to make her my own. Of course, in the beginning, the head below my waist was in control. I marked my territory so no one else could have her. It wasn't long before something else took over and the constant thought of "I want her" that runs through my mind started playing a different tune.

Maybe I'd gotten to the point in my life when easy pussy became boring. But I'd like to think better of myself. And I definitely think better of Kimber. If anyone was able to change me it was bound to be her.

I use my lower body to hold her against the stairwell wall.

"Ruin away." She dares me, raising a light sculpted

brow.

Kimber takes the temples of my black glasses frame between her fingers and removes them from my face.

Middle-class housewife isn't her usual attire. It's a turn-on nonetheless. Similar to her work clothes, these shorts cling to her ass in all the right places. My thumb sneaks past her khakis and up the thin navy blue shirt she's wearing, caressing the underside of her breast through her silky bra. When the light shone through the factory window, and she moved in the right direction, the fabric of her cotton top became translucent, showing me all the places I've skimmed my tongue against. I could stand seeing her looking like an ad for a southern department store more frequently. I'm intimately aware of what's underneath. My girl kept wearing G-strings for me long after she'd stopped stripping and started managing at Sweet Caroline's.

Our hungry lips crash together as if I haven't already kissed her half a dozen times this morning. I can't get enough of this woman.

Kimber claws at my back. I push her farther into the wall, sucking the soft spot behind her ear, and making her moan. I fucking love that sound falling from her lips when I'm buried balls deep inside her.

I'd slip my hand down her pants if this interlude wasn't messing up her timetable for the day. I've come to understand Kimber's desperation, why her kisses are more frenzied than they were an hour ago.

Before she left the second-floor lounge to get ready, it was closer to a typical Saturday morning for us. We'd sat on a sofa, drinking the steamy cups of Joe she'd poured. Uninterrupted by the sun or anyone else, my palm slid up the leg of her sleep pants, holding Kimber above the ankle while we talked quietly. We both knew deep down the calmness was about to change, but some things we don't say aloud. Most of them we don't need to.

What Kimber is feeling today is the same thing she endured a year ago and twelve months before that: A longing to be close, which I refuse to deny her. Drowning in emotions, she's searching for a life preserver. I'll wrap my arms around Kimber to keep her safe any damned way she pleases. I want to convince my fiery redhead that I'm her anchor.

Her personal convictions aside, it's finally the day she's got to let me give her everything I've always wanted to. Everything she lost and doesn't believe she'll find again. And if her heart hasn't mended? Well, that's on me. I have to admit to myself it might be time to tuck my tail between my legs. Although, I'm not sure how I'll walk away and leave her empty again.

I pull Kimber back to the center of the landing, straightening her clothes while I'm still kissing her. "You're going to be late, My Love." I grin between nips and bites.

She glances down, brushing her hands over the tats peeking out from my shirt collar, and tracing the lines of others on my pecs hidden by the fabric. "Can't blame a girl for losing her head over someone as sexy as you."

Using the tatted knuckle of my index finger, I lift her chin so our eyes meet. "Tell me again how much you want me?"

I chuckle when she slaps my chest. Unfortunately, I've got the same desire Kimber does. I'll never tire of hearing her say she wants to fuck me and only me. If she keeps it up today, it might change tomorrow for us.

"Sterling's?" I lace her dainty fingers through my rough ones and ask where we're going. The upscale engraving shop in North Hills is the place she's had me stop each year.

Her face breaks into a wide grin and she pats her purse. "Yes." I catch a little blush across her porcelain cheeks.

Kimber is my unbreakable China doll. She's been to

hell and found the determination to bring herself back. I can't fathom half of it considering her life—or rather ours since we've been together—is as close to perfection as I've been able to make it for her. That said, I'm the one who does everyone's background checks for Jake, the owner of Sweet Caroline's. Per Carver's instructions for anyone who he lets live at the mill, I also had to dig deeper. Nobody sticks around the factory unless we're sure they aren't inviting trouble to our door.

In Kimber's case, she was one of Jake's girls, attempting to take control of her life. He proposed Carver put her up on the third floor. The only dancers Carver does that for are the ones who are clean and stay clean. It doesn't matter none that they're stripping their way through Pinewood State. It's that those women want more for themselves than what life's thrown their way.

Spew any hateful thing about Carver and Jake. It's likely the truth, unless it comes to females. They only fuck over the women who fuck with them. It doesn't make them much different than any other man on the planet. The good girls like mine? They'll build a stairway to get those ladies to their goals.

The residents of the third floor all have skeletons in their closets. Kimber is no exception. She's also about five to ten years older than her floormates so she's had extra time for trouble to find her. Kinda like me. Only my sole purpose has become keeping her on the straight and narrow. I got fed up with finding trouble a long time ago. My job focuses on figuring out what kind of shit I can use, good or bad, against someone. The reason I don't need My Love to confess her transgressions is because I'm aware of what they are.

Chapter Three

Trig

"Woah." Kimber is at an utter loss for words as I hold open the door to Carver's new ride.

I slide behind the wheel. The dash is wood grain, and the buttery yellow leather seats are softer and more comfortable than anything else I've experienced. My bed at the end of a long day doesn't feel this plush.

"Makes sense why Jasper keeps stealing the thing when Carver is out of town. This car is the lap of fuckin' luxury."

"How did you get him to loan it to you for the entire day?

"He owes me a favor. Besides, you're meant to be riding in style." I wink. "Okay, Sterling's. Anyplace else?"

"I'd like an espresso if you think there's time." She bites her lower lip as if indulging her one vice is putting me out.

Morning, noon, and night Kimber survives on caffeine. She's also picky as hell about it. Iced; it's black because the cubes melt. Hot; she wants something sweet with it, but no sugar in it. Cream? Only enough to change the rich chocolate brown color to a dark tan. As far as dependencies go, I don't think I've ever seen her get the shakes or it stop her from falling asleep. I do worry about asking her to cut back. Or, God forbid, switch to decaf.

I'm more than agreeable to drop in at Baked Beans, her favorite coffee shop, as long as it's on my terms.

"Stay put," I tell her while I go inside to pick up the order she's placed on the drive over.

It's closing in on noon and her shift at Sweet Caroline's ended at three am. Kimber is never sure if Jake, who owns the place, will show his ugly mug on any given night. It doesn't seem to bug her any since Jake allows her free rein over whatever goes down at the strip club when they are open. She says it's easier without Jake around in the evenings. Kimber's only got so much patience for drunk patrons and Jake, like me, avoids calling the cops whenever possible. Luckily, a good number of men I trust work the door and barback for her. Businessmen are more intimidated by a rough, muscled guy with tight fists than the boys in blue with those cuffs attached to their belts. Kimber's learned to use it to her advantage. The dancers and female waitstaff also hassle her less if Jake's gone. Since Kimber worked the stage at Sweet Caroline's herself, she's good at tamping down the drama. I figure that's the key reason Jake's okay with handing over so much autonomy. He avoids dealing with everyone's shit at all costs. Along with basically any other human emotion. That's his problem, though. I don't poke my nose into any of my friend's business any further than I'm told to.

I've got the kind of job where you can make your own hours. It makes it easy for us to keep the same schedule. Each night, I go over to Jake's club at closing time to ensure the bar and the parking lot are empty. Then I walk Kimber across the street to the old cotton mill where we live so she gets home safely. The past few evenings, I've napped while she's been gone to be ready for her when she's back. It always takes Kimber a while to settle after work. The best way to send her off into dreamland is by wearing her out.

I may have put all my effort into that last night. We're running on little sleep and today is bound to be a long one for both of us.

I place two grandes in the cupholder and Kimber immediately goes after hers. "What did I do right to deserve you?"

"Everything." I remind her as if it's a joke. "Absolutely everything."

Kimber's fingertips play in my hair. Her forehead wrinkles as she tries not to frown. I lean in to kiss her before she can argue and turn a lighthearted moment on its ass. She needs as many of these as I can give her.

"Sterlings," I say with confidence, guiding the wheel across town to the upscale store.

A clerk in a deep-toned suit and tie takes the time to wipe any smudges from the frame before presenting it to Kimber for inspection. Each year she's gotten the same gift. A four-by-six silver picture frame engraved with the birthday girl's age. The swirling script this year reads: eighteen.

She pulls it to her chest and closes her eyes. Normally, I'd stand behind Kimber to be her rock. Today, I place a warm hand on her lower back. The reassurance is what she needs to flip the frame over, open the back, and unzip her purse. From an envelope, she pulls a time-worn picture and inserts it behind the glass.

I snag her wrist as she places it back into the box.

My breath leaves my body and there is an eerie stillness to the air. It's as if the other customers and clerks in the store move about while we're stuck in suspended animation. I draw Kimber's arm toward me, holding the frame closer to me for a clearer look.

She stares at the picture too, afraid of what she might see in my eyes. If the past four years have taught me anything, it's that Kimber's made of thicker stock. She steels herself and glances up. If I'd chosen now to condemn her, then she's better off without me.

"I don't think I've ever seen you look more beautiful." From the shimmer in her eyes, I can tell Kimber understands I mean it.

"What I would have given to hear a man say those words to me on the day the picture was taken." She confesses, for the first time opening up to me about an old wound.

The clerk re-shines, re-boxes, and gift wraps the frame with pink wrapping and an organdy bow. The oval Sterling's sticker brings back my comment about having the finer things in life. I hope the birthday girl understands why Kimber bought it at this store.

Of course she can, I reassure myself. She's eighteen, about to graduate high school, and go on to college. Doubting her intelligence would be like doubting Kimber's determination.

Back in Carver's car, we drive without directions from Kimber or the GPS. I park on the opposite side of the street from the house, cut the engine, and leave the blower on to keep me cool.

"I can call for an U—"

"I insist on waiting right here." I cross my arms so she can't fight. There's no use. She'd lose anyway. This has been where I've stayed each year while she's at the party. I'll never ask to go in. She's never asked permission to bring me along. This part of her life has had to remain separate or the gaping hole wouldn't have healed at all.

Chapter Four

Kimber

"Kimber! You're here." Aidy flings the front door open and is running from the front porch toward me as soon as I step foot out of the car. Her arms wrap around my neck. I move her gift out of the way, hugging her back. We sink together, holding on for the same slim second extra that I'd held her in my arms on the day she was born.

"I wouldn't miss today for anything, Dumplin'." It's true. I've been through hell and high water to be here.

"Did you always call me that?" She's whispered the same words ever since she was old enough to understand who I was.

"From the very beginning," I rub her back so she knows how much she's always been cherished. My fingertips play between her long, poker-straight, red strands of hair cascade down. Aidy came into this world bald as a ping-pong ball, leaving me wondering what she'd look like.

While I couldn't name my daughter, I could call her something special. As soon as my belly began rising she became my Dumplin'.

I grab her hands, hold them wide, and look at the reflection of an eighteen-year-old me. Sure, the shape of her eyes is the same as *his* were, and she got stuck with *his* mismatched earlobes—one's attached, the other isn't. But the rest? That's my baby. He didn't want her, so I get to claim every other feature Aidy has.

"I think you're more of a biscuit since you're all grown up now." I joke, cautiously.

Aidy laughs, glancing at her form.

"Never." I wink. "You're far too slim. Besides," I spin for her. "What you see is what you'll get."

My family is slender right up until sixty-something. I may not have been kind to the years, but the years have been kind to me. I'm not ready to freak out about how my torso will change, and I certainly don't want Aidy concerned about her body image. Lord knows I deal with female self-consciousness enough at Sweet Caroline's when the dancers complain they are bloated.

"I like this top." She compliments me.

I say a small thanks, grateful I'll fit in with the rest of the guests. It's hard to be myself and someone's biological mother. I'd worry less about Aidy's impression of me had I raised her.

"Hey, you're right on time." A strong hand grips my shoulder.

"Hi, Don." I give a sheepish smile to Aidy's dad. "I'll only stick around a bit."

"You feed us the same line each year, Kimber. But you stay. And we're glad you do."

"My turn." Ghillie, Aidy's mom, steps in. She clasps my cheeks and we stare at one another. Her blue eyes water. Ghillie has short black hair and, oddly enough, the freckles Aidy and I don't have despite being gingers. I've always been acutely aware that Ghillie's not me. Yet, she's the only mother my daughter has ever known.

"We did it." Ghillie's gracious reaction to today is how I was positive she was the one for Aidy. The person to take my place and love her like nobody else. I'm not certain I could have been strong enough to live with the ghost of my child's birth mother lingering throughout her childhood. Let alone find the kindness to include them.

"The credit goes to you and Don! You were the parents there every day, not me."

I cried losing her, but my daughter grew up in suburbia surrounded by people who wanted her. I couldn't have given Aidy half the opportunities Don and Ghillie did. Child protective services probably would have taken Aidy away from me anyhow. Her first chance with them was the best chance at a better life.

"You forget, the three of us wouldn't be standing here at all if it weren't for you, Kimber. I wouldn't be her mom if it—Thank you." She chokes.

I use the back of my hand to wipe the tears streaming down my cheeks. "Ghillie, we're both going to be a wreck if we can't keep the waterworks at bay for another few hours."

"Oh." She fans her face. "Let everyone look. Let 'em say we're being sentimental fools. Aidy is eighteen today. We're allowed to be proud and cry happy tears." Ghillie spies the pink box I'm holding. "Would you like me to take that?"

"Uh, yes. But I have to warn you: It's different this year."

"She loves the pictures of you when you were her age, Kimber. They sit with her trophies and awards. Sharing this part of you with her…Well, those frames are some of Aidy's most prized possessions."

"Thank you for saying that. I still need to tell you; she's in this one. I mean, not as a baby. It was taken right before she was born. I don't want you to think I'd want her to— "

Ghillie touches my arm. "I'll put it in Aidy's room and open it with her tonight."

I do my best impression of a wallflower watching Aidy with her friends. She's so happy and carefree. Not at all how I was at her age. I ended my senior year of high school in the maternity ward. Now, I worry that I should have given her the picture of us right after she was born instead. It's selfish of me to keep the sole copy I have.

A few of her aunts and uncles who are here know who I am. None of them are rude to me. We talk around my connection with the family as if it doesn't exist. This is Aidy's special day, and Don and Ghillie's as well. I won't ruin it by drawing unwanted attention to myself. I enjoy getting caught up listening to conversations about what Aidy has done over the past year. The itty-bitty insights into her life make me feel like I know her better than I do.

A neighbor whom I've never met has been chasing a toddler around the house. She finally gives up, puts her hands on her hips, and talks to me about her little boy. Aidy is his babysitter.

"We're going to miss her so much when she goes off to Pinewood State." She glances at her son who has planted himself in Aidy's lap while she chats with her girlfriends. "Friday nights won't be the same. Do you have any kids, Kimber?"

The woman returns her gaze to me and recognition flashes across her face.

"No," I reply in a flat tone, unwilling to reveal more about myself than is necessary to a stranger.

I swirl my sweet tea, wishing it was brewed from beans instead of leaves, and watching the ice melt. I stopped lying to myself around this time last year. I'd like a family of my own. A little house. A second chance. But I only want those things if Trig is part of the equation. We're open about everything but Aidy.

I'm not sure how to tell him how I feel without bringing this situation into the mix. I also haven't been completely truthful with him. Deep down I'm frightened if I do, then the silly belief things will work out for us isn't true.

The conversation with the neighbor becomes awkward. She ducks out, interested in getting the little boy home for a nap, though I doubt the child needs one.

The next hour ticks by at an agonizing pace. All of a sudden, no matter who speaks to me, I'm the odd-woman out. I'd like to find a quiet corner to cry in and a hot cup of coffee to do it in.

Toward the end of the afternoon, the candles on Aidy's cake are lit. Everyone in the room begins singing. Ghillie holds back Aidy's hair. It's the same shade as the flames. Don is about to snap a picture and Aidy beckons me over to stand by her side before bending to blow them out.

"You belong with Ghillie." I take the camera from him so that he'll take the place next to Aidy.

"Only if the next snapshot is of Aidy with you." He shuffles behind the dining room table.

I press the shutter so it goes off several times in succession. Then I lay the camera on the table and scoot out of the room before anyone can switch places. There's only one picture of me with my daughter, and it's the one I keep.

Chapter Five

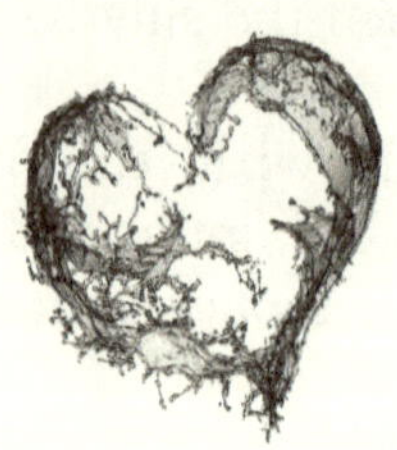

Trig

A knock on the window has me cracking an eye. I've been minding my own business for the past three hours while Kimber's been at the party. I'd scrolled my feed and returned a few calls. Then, deciding—after a long night of making love to my woman and knowing she'll need me to take care of her and do the same this evening—it was in my best interest to get twenty winks. I've been relaxing against the buttery leather of Carver's car. The heated seat massages my back and cool air flowing from the air conditioner floats over me. It's like being down at the Crystal Coast on a clear day with the breeze blowing off the ocean while the hot sand radiates through your beach towel.

The tapping on the glass has me prepared to choke whatever idiot thinks they can piss at me for loitering. It's a public street, not a no-parking zone. I'm channeling a decent amount of Zen. However, there's also a part of me that's anxious, ready to beat up any stupid fucker who tries to insinuate I'm here to case the neighborhood. Little do they know I have the cash to pay off the mortgages of every goddamn house on the cul-de-sac flat out. I'd give Kimber the pick of the litter. Hell, she could have one for each day.

Lost in thought, I'm as shocked at the grin spreading across my face as anyone. Kimber's standing in the grass, wiggling her fingers. She has on a tentative smile. The softness of her gaze, though like I'm the one person who can make everything she's feeling all better, has a sunny warmth spreading to my chest.

I unlock the doors and roll down the window in a smooth motion.

"Party over, My Love?"

"I'm all set to go. Thank you for waiting. I didn't mean to stay the whole time." Every year she apologizes without need.

I'd never deny her those few hours with her daughter. In fact, I'd drive her here and nap by the curb every weekend, if Don and Ghillie allowed Kimber to see Aidy the way divorced parents shared joint custody. I'm no fool. It doesn't work like that with adoption. But if I have one wish for Kimber—outside of the things I want *with* her—it's now that Aidy's come of age and able to make her own choices, they'll form a friendship.

Kimber walks around the hood of the car, getting in the passenger side, and buckling up. She folds her hands in her lap, sighing, and pursing her lips. It's not unusual for Kimber to stare out the window unspeaking while we drive home. I let her have her space. She's aware of the tears falling down her cheeks. I don't tell her she's crying or ask her why.

But unlike every other year, before I can put the sedan into gear, her hands fly to her face and Kimber crumbles. She's used up her stoic strength. Eighteen years of putting on a brave front is enough for her.

"I wanted her so much, Trig," Kimber confesses.

I pull her as close to me as the center console will allow, stroking her long red hair. It may be different between a parent and child, but I understand the desire to keep someone in your life. This is the first time Kimber has ever acknowledged to me that Aidy is her daughter. I've respected her privacy and won't push her for details, even though as soon as Kimber opened her mouth, I was flooded with the need to know the full story.

I'm forced to admit the way she's relied on me isn't enough. It's time for her to stop carrying this burden alone. If I am her man, I'm the one she should rely on when it's too hard to go on anymore. The weight of her pain I will gladly bear.

"He didn't want her at all. I was a teenager, on my own as soon as my mother found out, with no future. I had nothing to give a baby. I could hardly feed myself, let alone her."

Kimber pulls away. I sense her closing up. The admission is overwhelming. She licks her dry lower lip and I wipe her tears away with my thumbs. More spring up in their place. The outlandish concern that I'd think less of her overshadows her need to continue.

"Don't be scared. There's nothing you can say that will ever change the way I feel about you. You could climb out of this car, slamming the door behind you, and never look back, and my sorry ass will pine for you, My Love." I brush a lock of hair behind her ear. "All your strength and devotion keeps my world from tumbling off its axis. I don't thank you near as much as I should for making me a good man... Or at least making me feel like I am one."

"I owe you the truth," Kimber says, her obligations to the past a debt that's paid.

"You don't owe me shit. I may want to know, but it doesn't mean the rest of your story is mine for the taking."

"I'm ready to tell it."

"Want to go someplace more private?" There are

other guests leaving Don and Ghillie's, heading to their cars.

"I might lose my nerve."

Nobody has more backbone than Kimber. But I'm not taking the chance. I settle back in the seat, letting her drive the conversation.

Chapter Six

Kimber

Trig presses a kiss to my fingertips. He sits back in the seat. Carver's gorgeous car contrasts my ugly tale about how I got stuck watching a precious baby girl grow up from a distance.

The man I love holds my hand. His willingness to let me lay my truths at his feet is scary as hell. But somehow I'm assured he won't stomp on them, leaving my heart splintered the way Aidy's father had.

My pulse pounds in my ear. I've gone over every memory in my head a million times. I've thought of telling Trig a thousand of those.

"He was just a boy, and I was just a girl. We met at school. He took me on dates and to the prom. It was normal. I believed him when he said he loved me. There was no reason not to. I won't tell you it was a lie to get in my pants. At that age, all you know of love is what you're experiencing. I don't doubt he cared, nor do I discount when he found out I was pregnant that he was as scared as I was. Whatever love he had for me got lost in his fear. He left, leaving the rest up to me." The eighteen-year-old who still lives deep inside thirty-six-year-old me shrugs.

"All I had was a fast food job. It wasn't enough to live on or afford..." My voice trails. There were times I considered the mental anguish of not having my baby at all would have been better for me than letting her go. That didn't happen until after she'd been born and I'd already made a very final choice.

Trig's steel eyes bore into mine. He knows what I'm thinking. "No judgment. Not even if you'd made a different choice from the get-go."

The confidence he has in me makes it easier to go on.

"Ghillie and Don went to the same church we did. I'd never met them, but she was so pretty, and the way Don seemed captivated by her made them stand out. They didn't have kids, which didn't make sense to me. The nurse at the clinic I was going to gave me some brochures. When I got the nerve to call one of the adoption counselors, I was shocked to find their profile in the albums at the center's offices."

The events come out backward. Trig doesn't seem to mind the way I connect the dots.

"They'd been on the list a long time. 'Forever' Ghillie said when I let them know I'd chosen her and Don to be my baby's parents. They were okay with an open adoption. I wanted to be in Aidy's life and believed this way I'd be assured she was safe and have pictures of her growing up.

"But toward the end of my pregnancy, I wasn't mature enough to handle it. I told Ghillie in no uncertain terms she couldn't be there when Aidy was born. It had to be her and me. I didn't want anyone else ruining the moment. We originally agreed they could come get her right afterward, but I forced them to wait until I left the hospital so I had more time with my baby."

"That's not wrong, Kimber. Don and Ghillie had the

next eighteen years. One day, two days? You don't think you deserved time to bond with Aidy?"

"That's the problem. I did bond with her and I didn't want to give her up." Ashamed, I direct my line of vision to the fire hydrant on the corner, willing it to explode.

I inhale, ready to tell Trig the worst part. "No contact for the first two years... I mean, I got pictures. Reminders she was living the life she was meant to without me. And, stupid me, I knew where Don and Ghillie lived. So each time the mail showed, I'd go to their house and try to sneak a glance at my baby girl. When I handed her over, I didn't even know what color hair she'd have, and all I wanted was a real-life glimpse of her soft red curls..."

"Kimber, you didn't?"

"Nuh-uh, what I did was worse than trying to get her back. I started drinking, which led to drugs. On Aidy's third birthday, they finally allowed me to see her. Every year after, I'd get myself cleaned up, so it didn't show and I got a few minutes with her. Until the pain I felt when I saw how good she had it, and how horrible her life would have been with me, was too much. I stopped coming to see her each year for a while. I was too busy throwing a pity party of my own."

"Did you ever ask yourself if it was the postpartum thing?"

"In hindsight, it was. But back then? Who treated a teenage girl who'd gotten herself in trouble and given her baby up for adoption for depression? I was told I was lucky Don and Ghillie were allowing me to be a small part of Aidy's life. All those experienced adults directed my actions. They made me believe my private thoughts made me an ingrate when I was grateful. Aidy's parents are wonderful people. It's why I chose them."

Trig's lip twitches, curling at the side into a small

smile. I don't have to ask if he's done background checks on them. I'm sure he's privy to far more about Don and Ghillie than I ever was when the adoption agency handed me their profile two decades ago.

"By then, I was, uh, living with this girl. She was using too and started turning tricks to afford her addictions. I won't ever pretend I didn't sleep with someone to get high, Trig. My pride won't let me. But she wound up pregnant and the writing on the wall was sobering. I'd already given up one baby. A second would kill me long before I overdosed. I beat myself up because Aidy was living without me, instead of making a life she'd understand and be proud of me for. It struck me how someday I'd be dead and my daughter would believe I threw her away; that getting high was more important to me than she was. I'd never have a chance to explain. She'd only see addiction as my weakness when it was really her all along.

"So I stumbled flat on my face into sobriety." I'm around free-flowing alcohol at Sweet Caroline's and there's plenty of it at the mill.

Trig nods. "Your unwillingness to even enjoy a glass of wine on girls' night or have a beer with me made it much harder to convince you to come to my bed."

"Now you get why." I let out a strangled laugh and begin wringing my hands.

"Hey," he says. "I just don't ever want you missing out on having a good time. I understood why all along and didn't mind working a little harder. The first time with you was magic. Why do you think I haven't let you leave since?"

"Thanks," I say, barely audible. "I love you."

Rubbing my knee, he whispers the same words back.

Chapter Seven

Trig

We'd stayed parked on the street for a while with Kimber revealing her truths. I asked questions because I was glad we were finally communicating about this. It opens the door for other things. I also hadn't wanted her to clam up, believing my opinion of her had swayed. Or worse, if I remained silent it meant I was disinterested in her past. Some of what she said I'd always wanted to know. But again, it was her private business, not mine to nose into.

The car was running on fumes when we pulled away from the curb to go get gas. I'd have figured Kimber was running on empty too. However, she kept talking. Little smiles played at the corners of the lips as her life turned around. I liked that a heck of a lot more than hearing about her struggles.

Fuck, if I didn't want to find Aidy's birth father and beat the shit out of the guy for stranding Kimber. Or go back in time and make sure *I* was her boyfriend instead. I might have been up to no good, but I'm sure as shit positive that the last thing I would have done was leave

Kimber high and dry, pregnant with my baby. Like I said, the first damned thing that floated through my brain when I laid eyes on Kimber was that I was determined to make her mine. I don't doubt had I met her as a teenager those same words would have brought us together.

I listened intently as she told me about her sponsor and the program.

"That's about the time I started dancing. I was still young enough to pull it off and guess the shame about being naked in front of people isn't half of what I'd already felt. I'd been at another club and one of the girls, who was way younger than me, was using her income to pay for college. I was making enough that it made sense. I wasn't the dumbest girl in school, even if I hadn't made the wisest choices. Jake saw me and offered a spot in his revue with a raise. How was I supposed to say no?"

"Cuz he comes off as a complete jerk." I'd snorted.

"You'll never understand what dreams someone's lost out on until you get to know the real person."

"Don't let Jake hear you talking kind about him. He's worked hard to garner his reputation."

"Turtles are soft under that hard shell."

I raise a brow.

"Well, they are. My point is everybody has armor."

"You're right." I conceded, kissing the back of her hand before I got out to pump gas.

Kimber was closing the mirror and flipping up the visor when I shifted the car back into drive.

"I look a wreck." She flopped against the seatback.

"You're beautiful. I was searching for a way of getting that makeup off your face anyhow."

She huffed like she didn't believe me, but out of the corner of my eye I saw her blush.

I pull Carver's car up to the rear of the three-story building and hit the button for the bay door to garage it. I have to be honest, I'll be sorry giving the keys back to him. Watching My Love open up and let me into her past made me realize she should have more nice things. Creature comforts. Maybe a sweet ride after the roller coaster these past eighteen years were for her.

I'll be repaying my buddy for his generosity. Not only for allowing me to use his vehicle, but for inviting Kimber to live at the mill. It's our home. Though, I'd prefer not for much longer.

She lets out a ragged breath, taking the words on the tip of my tongue right out of my mouth. "Don't get me wrong, everyone here is special to me, Trig. But I can't deal with them tonight. Does it make me a bad person?"

"Not at all. It's okay to need space. Grab the bag. Let's go for a ride." My Harley is parked next to Skye and Jasper's by the garage. We ride together. It's not a club like Jasper's sister, Sloan freaked out about. I do enough other illegal shit that it doesn't leave time for running guns. Smoking pot? If Kimber's not around. I won't bring any of that crap around her. It's not fair to ask of an addict. I've known she'd struggled from the beginning.

"How far can we make it tonight?"

"Depends on which direction you'd like to go in. The beach? Mountains?" Blowing Rock is a good three hours from here. That may be a trek.

It doesn't take the rumble of my stomach to tell she's aware I've missed lunch. Not that my bastard gut cares as it lets out the gurgle.

"We could go for dinner and turn around and come back once we know everyone is asleep." Kimber's white face turns green. It doesn't seem as if she wants to eat. Or come home. I can't blame her.

I haven't had much in the line of sustenance today. It hits a little spot that she doesn't want to put me out. We keep a to-go bag ready for the times the walls at the factory close in on us. It's a simple backpack with an extra set of clothes. Kimber drops the few extra toiletries we need in depending on where we plan on winding up. The destination I have in mind is special.

"I know a place. You go change and pack us up. Toothbrushes included. We're not coming back tonight."

And if I can help it, the next time we're back at the factory, it won't be for long.

Chapter Eight

Kimber

"We have a room here?" I take off my helmet in awe of the tall white columns and wraparound porch of the old manor inn.

The mill where we live is pretty darn nice accommodations. Yet, this isn't any place like we'd normally stay on the road. It doesn't slip past me that this is an upscale bed and breakfast.

I'd changed into dark jeans before we left the mill. Both Trig and I wear our leather jackets early fall through late spring unless the heat is excruciating. The helmets stop bugs from getting in our teeth, but right now I feel woefully underdressed.

"What is this place?" I pluck a beetle that didn't make it from Trig's open collar and say a little prayer before dropping him in the grass.

"It's like an event place with nice hotel rooms. They hold weddings out back and have a gourmet restaurant. I made overnight reservations while you were getting our stuff together," Trig removes the light backpack from my shoulders, sliding it over his and takes my helmet.

I'm forever amazed at how his wide grip holds the cumbersome weight of both.

"You mind if we have dinner before checking into our room?"

"Oh, I don't mind." I shake my head—feeling like Alice getting her first glimpse at her garden surroundings—and reenter the real world. "We can go to the restaurant first." I've forgotten my manners. Trig hasn't eaten since breakfast. He must be starved.

Wide old wooden steps creak under our boots. The smell wafting out to the porch as Trig holds the door for me is amazing. I picked at the party buffet earlier, not in the mood to fill my belly. Now, after about two hours on the road, I'm feeling better, more like eating.

First, we wound westward over the back roads out of Brighton, enjoying the scenery. Then Trig hopped on I-85 north of Durham. With my thighs pressed to his ass and my arms wrapped around his sides, the wind rushed by us. The hum of the bike's engine underneath and the closeness of his body brought our conversation in the car to completion.

Not wanting to stay home tonight aside, I've never wanted to escape my past. My journey made me who I am, and I have pride in me the way I want Aidy to be proud. However, with everything out in the open, I'm freer and able to move on.

Trig requests a table for two. The hostess is gracious given our appearance.

We both slide off our jackets, trying to blend in with the other diners. When Trig goes to hide our helmets and bag under the tablecloth, the hostess offers to keep them up at her station.

"Not a big deal." Trig tries to wave her off. "I've got a room booked."

"I'd be glad to bring them up there if you'd like," she says, full of kindness and hospitality. "Give me a few minutes and I'll bring you back the key. I'll even check you in while you're waiting for your meal. The inn does things the old fashioned way. We don't have much in terms of computers. I'll need you to fill out your room card—in pen." She laughs at the antiquated methods of the past with a mock eye roll.

Trig allows the hostess to take our backpack and helmets. She juggles them the way I would. Not long after the server brings out a beer for Trig and a coffee for me, Trig has signed the card and we're ordering.

Seated across the table from one another, Trig and I hold hands. His fingertip nudges underneath my cuff bracelet and I take it off as a matter of habit. His brows slam together and he frowns. It's not until then when I remember the bruise.

Did I do that? Trig's harsh expression judges his own demons and pleads for it not to be the truth.

"It looks worse than it is. It's not painful." Knowing it would be a long ride, I'd snagged ibuprofen to be sure my wrist wouldn't lock up while we were on the highway.

Trig sighs heavily, refusing to meet my eyes. He's ashamed of himself, and he shouldn't be.

"It's not your fault," I whisper. "It's never your fault, My Love. You don't even know it's happening."

"How many times have you hidden it from me, Kimber?" Trig scrubs his face.

I reach out to cup his cheek, forcing his steely eyes to mine. "Only today. There was too much going on. I'd forgotten about it, and the sweatshirt I had on over my pajamas hid it from me. I didn't even notice until I got out of the shower this morning."

My big man's jaw ticks, trying to hold back his emotions. He's shattered every time this happens. Yet, it's never been as bad as the night he clocked me with his fist hard enough that no amount of makeup could hide the shiner he gave me. Most of the problem stemmed from when Carver saw me. He didn't understand, and he threatened Trig's life should he put his hands on me again.

World War three almost broke out at the mill. Carver has no tolerance for violence against women. He was ready to ban us from the guy's rooms the same way he refuses to allow men on the third floor. Even the exception he made for Trig rides a very fine line for him. Trig had to get a psych eval from the VA and he still goes to therapy.

It may seem like the people I surround myself with have no conscience, and maybe there are times that rings true. But, in reality, their hearts bleed like everyone else's.

Trig grasps his palm over the Airborne tat on his arm. He'd enlisted and served out of Fort Bragg. His military career ended post two tours overseas. He's been honest about what he saw in Afghanistan and how being in a war zone affected him.

The things Trig experienced in combat have settled on the periphery of his mind. He doesn't dwell. It's not unlike the way I handle my feelings about Aidy. Except, whenever Trig is troubled, he has awful dreams. He jerks beside me, holding on for dear life, grappling with the loss of friends, and survivor syndrome. I'm glad to be his anchor and understand that if he could stop this, he would. Trig never intends to hurt me.

Chapter Nine

Trig

In our hotel room, Kimber lies unashamed of her body on the white sheets. They're the same shade as the whipped cream that was on the dessert we shared, and she's as delectable. My fingers tickle her navel and an easy smile plays on her lips. I shimmy down the bed so her tummy is even with my head and lean on my elbow, caressing the softest parts of my woman. I dip my lips forward, trailing them across the solitary, three-inch, silvery line stretching from her pelvic bone to her hip. She's tried to hide the beauty of it with Aidy's name in a swirling font. Two little footprints are inked after the "y". The scar, tattoo, and wound on her heart are delicate. The same as Kimber. But I haven't once doubted her strength. You don't do what she did for her kid without a shit ton of backbone.

I feather kisses against the tiny feet, steeling myself for her honest answer to the one question I haven't had the spine to ask. I don't think I'll like her response. As a matter of fact, I've always believed it would lead to our demise. That's why I haven't pushed. Why I haven't had the balls to bring it up until now. I don't want to be without Kimber, but we can't go on the way we are. Something's gotta change.

"Would you do it again?" I can hardly hear my voice despite the quiet of the room.

Kimber shakes her head sadly, but responds, "For her, yes."

"That's not what I'm asking you, My Love. Your regrets when it comes to Aidy aren't any of my business to judge. And unless you care to share any more of the story with me, I'd never consider interrupting the way you've chosen to heal."

Kimber touches the stubble on my cheek, taking in a heavy breath as if my words are ones she's been waiting to have confirmed.

I push up onto my wrists and lower myself back down on both elbows, placing my body over Kimber's, protectively caging her in. I bite my lip the way she does before voicing what I need. "Would you have another baby?"

Kimber blinks. Her pretty little lips form an "o".

"Now that she's grown?" I add. I've waited because it seems like this chapter of Kimber's life needed to end.

Her blue eyes dart to the closed curtains. "I didn't know you wanted kids," she says with contrition.

"With you, I want it all. I want to come home at night to a house in whatever suburb you please, to see you standing on the front porch with our baby on your hip and my ring on your finger. I don't call you 'My Love' for any reason other than it's what you are. You freely gave every ounce of love you deserved from Aidy to Ghillie and Don. It was at so much cost to your heart. I just wanna fill that well back up."

"Why didn't you tell me this sooner?"

"It wasn't the right time."

"And it is now that my daughter is an adult?"

"It is. If you'll have me."

"If not? Are we over? Is this an ultimatum?"

Feeling the rush of wind before seeing the light of the train, I shift to slide back to my side of the bed. Kimber holds my hip and tents her leg, stopping me from going too far.

Her fingers find my face again. I'm captivated by the faint glimmer in her eyes. It's similar to the one I've been hiding from her every time I've envisioned what it would be like hearing her say a test came back positive and that we were in this for life.

"I'd never force you to stay." I grunt.

I might. Perhaps not before when I didn't have the balls to admit this to Kimber. But now that it's out in the open? Fuck, I'm coming up with a million reasons to stop her from leaving. If she goes, then every hope and dream I had for the future disappears. Every minute spent waiting for today was a waste.

I could have found someone else. No, that's a lie. I couldn't. She is My Love. And I won't love anyone else the way I love Kimber ever again.

"I would have been wrong to force you to stay," she says, knocking me out of my thoughts, and away from the juvenile schemes I'm not above using to salvage our relationship.

"Trig, are you listening to me?"

On baited fucking breath.

"If you want a baby, we just stop using those." Kimber points to the used condom wrapper on the nightstand.

I shake my head. There must be something I'm missing.

"I haven't been on birth control for a while now. You always took care of it and I," she pauses, guilt flashing across her face. "I figured on the off chance that you didn't and something happened... Then if you didn't want it... Well, I'd figure it out." Kimber keeps babbling and I'm desperate to see where her thoughts have taken her. "It wasn't to trap you and I didn't expect it would be easy on my own. But I have a degree and a job now—even if it is at Sweet Caroline's—and I wouldn't have asked you for anything."

"You didn't expect me to stand by you?"

"*He* didn't. It scared me to tell him. You? I kept imagining you getting excited, and I told myself it was a fallacy. I was prepared for you to say it was my fault. I mean, I didn't tell you I wasn't on the pill anymore." She frowns and her shrug is caught by the pillowcase.

"So you're saying to me for the past year or so, you've wanted a baby and I've wanted a baby and we've both been too damned stubborn to let the other one know."

"Yeah?" She questions me back to make sure I'm not pissed as hell. It's so damned cute all I can do is steal a kiss.

"You're not mad?"

"At myself, cuz who the hell wants to wear a rubber if they can be knocking someone up instead?"

My response makes her laugh. Our mouths side together. I lick the seam of her lips and Kimber opens for me. I kiss her long and lazy, the same way I plan on making love to her until the sun comes up.

"Tell me next time. I won't break you trying to make you share anything weighing on you. It's not my way, Kimber. I steal facts about a person's life, and because of this, I won't read into emotions. I can't convince myself that I'm a good man if, trying to gather what you need to keep private, I wind up prying. Promise me if it's something like this—something about us or our kids—you'll come to me. I don't ever want to hurt you, intentionally or by accident."

"You could have made me a momma by now if I'd spoken up." Her eyes are watery, but her understanding is clear.

"Mmm, My Love, don't underestimate yourself. Mothers are the most giving people on the planet. What we need to get to work on is making me a daddy."

Chapter Ten

Kimber

My breath gets caught in my throat as Trig's tongue slides along my hip bone.

"If it's the last thing I do, I'm making sure you get a matching tattoo right here, My Love. Two more footprints and a name to carry with you," he says with reverence.

"Only one name? What if I want a belly covered in them?

"I will fill you up as many times as you let me." He stares up at me under hooded eyes, stroking the underside of my leg with his large hand.

I've made love to this man a million times. We've done dirty, unspeakable things to one another. Touching one another in hedonist ways that lay our vulnerabilities on the table plain for each other to see. The trust it takes making a baby with Trig is the most vulnerable I'll ever be. He knows this. It's why he waited to ask. What's more, I know part of biding his time was for my daughter. Aidy won't see this child as competition. Not that she should. Nothing compares to her and the love I have for her.

At the same time, not a damned thing will ever come close to the love I have for Trig. He put us first. Kept his life on hold. That's not easy for people our age.

My eyes flutter closed as Trig's beard scrapes the apex of my sex. My legs fall open, giving him access while his hands grip the globes of my ass. Trig presses his thumbs into my flesh to hold me steady. He swirls his tongue around my clit and I let out a whine. My hips lift, trying not to lose the connection with his mouth.

"Oh, my needy girl, I've already told you I'm giving you everything. Don't go getting impatient with me when I've been the one waiting."

"Please, Trig. I'm ready. I'm so, so ready."

"Not yet." he teases, sucking the sensitive skin on my upper thigh. His hand kneads my breast, tweaking the nipple. I take my breasts in my palms and Trigs fingertips skitter down, sliding inside of me. My pussy clenches and Trig draws the orgasm out of me.

"That's it, My Love. We're going to remember tonight."

His body rises to cover mine. Trig pushes my knees to either side. "Wide." He uses a single word direction. "I'm so hard for you it hurts." Trig enters me skin to skin for the first time with one smooth stroke.

"Oh, God." I mumble as our bodies move in unison. If this is heaven, I'm for damn sure never stepping one foot in hell again. Everything Trig says and does to me is perfect. And it dawns on me it's because he knows me inside and out. He patched up my heart, holding it close to his own hoping one day I'd recognize it wasn't a splintered mess anymore.

Trig

I silence my phone alarm before the classic rock playlist blares. We have to vacate our hotel room soon. I've been awake a few minutes already, twirling a loop of Kimber's long red hair between my fingers. From the way she's curled up in a fetal position at my side, it's obvious she needs a few more Zs.

Careful not to disturb her, I shimmy out from under the warm blankets and scratch below the belt, wordlessly telling my dick it needs to knock it off. He's had enough for now. We've got important shit to do today if we're bringing a baby into this world.

My muscles pop and I stretch to loosen up before we ride back. Grabbing my glasses from the nightstand, I turn toward the John. I give Kimber a few more minutes to recharge while I use the bathroom and find my pants and shirt.

For the first time in a week, I slept like a log. I could have been the sexfest, which wore me out. But I have a feeling it's more that I'm no longer worried about what direction our relationship is headed in. In fact, I know right where we belong and hope she agrees.

"Come on, sleepyhead." I kneel on the bed. Slipping my arms around Kimber from behind, I cup under her breasts and drag her up into a seated position. Her back rests against my chest.

"Five more minutes?" Her head falls forward. She lets out a contented sigh when my index finger grazes her supple nipple.

I sit back down, wrapping my legs around her and giving her the time she's requested. Her ass crack cradles what is left of my morning wood. I wait for Kimber to come awake and rub her sleepy blue eyes.

She stretches, intentionally brushing against my dick.

"We don't got time for that, My Love." I pinch her nipples, leaving Kimber in anticipation. For the number of times I came inside her last night, I'm pretty damned sure I'll have her knocked up soon. I'll also have her laid out on my bed later on to make sure of it.

I tug my sweatshirt over her head and toss her the pair of tight jeans, which she uses to hide her long creamy legs under. Such a fucking shame. I love those legs, especially when they're wrapped around me.

"Coffee." She yawns, lifting her arms over her head.

"I have just enough time to get you fed at the restaurant downstairs before we need to get a move on to meet the realtor."

I flick the screen on my phone and turn it toward her.

Kimber's big blue eyes pop open. She reaches for my cell, her jaw dropping lower than it had when she was waking up. "Is this—"

For us.

For real.

Forever.

All of the above and a hell of a lot more.

"Do you like it?" I ask her as she sinks to the bed, scrolling for the location and specs. "We'll need a place to bring 'em home to." And it sure as hell isn't going to be Carver's mill. "I'm not interested in waiting until we know for certain you're pregnant."

"I love it. I love you, Trig."

Epilogue

Kimber

"You're such a heartbreaker!" My nineteen-year-old daughter cuddles Owen, my infant son, close to her chest as we cross the threshold into Ghillie and Don's house.

Trig has an empty baby carrier in one hand and an overflowing diaper bag slung over his shoulder.

"Can we keep him? I want one so bad!" Aidy squeals like it has been more than a week since she's babysat for Trig and me.

"NO!" All four of us yell in unison.

Our shouts startled the baby. He frowns and fusses.

"I was kidding!" she says, bouncing Owen. "Wasn't I?" She coos, trying to settle him. "Wasn't I? I could eat you up." She nibbles his cheek.

Owen smiles, making a silly baby laugh. They disappear to a couch in the living room to bond.

"Nobody else is here yet?" I question, placing Aidy's birthday present on the kitchen counter.

Ghillie makes an *mm-mh* sound. "This year she only wanted her family here, especially that baby brother of hers. She's been planning this for weeks, Kimber, since you and Trig let her visit you in the hospital when Owen was born." Ghillie pauses, looking uncertain. "It's not uncomfortable, is it? Aidy isn't forcing herself on you?" Her voice comes out a whisper.

"Not at all. I've worried about the opposite. That you feel like we're encroaching on your life."

Ghillie places her hand on her heart. "You gave us your baby and then gave our daughter the baby brother she wanted. Aidy is doing amazing in college. Though, I'm sure she'll tell you all about it. What I'm trying to say is, she's happy. What else can I ask for my child?"

"I'm so glad to hear that." I touch Ghillie's arm. "But, for what it's worth, in my eyes, you'll always be her mom. I'd never take back what I gave you or ruin those memories."

"I know you wouldn't. It's why you stayed away during the years when life was rougher for you. You trusted us enough to love her when you couldn't." Ghillie stops. I can see her searching for the right words so she doesn't offend me. "This may come out snotty, but I don't doubt my relationship with Aidy. When things go wrong for her, I'm the person she comes to. But you and Trig are her family too. And, once I'm done washing these vegetables, I plan to go steal Owen from her to get my own snuggles in before dinnertime. He's beautiful. Just like Aidy was. Don and I are so happy for you and Trig."

"Thank you." I wipe the tears pooling under my eyes and curse my hormones.

Trig holds Owen through dinner until I've cleaned my plate. Then we switch off so he can eat while I feed the baby.

Aidy brings her cake to the table when we're finished, and Ghillie asks if we'd like coffee with dessert.

"Decaf?" I question.

I'm certain I was pregnant on the ride back to the

mill. Kicking my caffeine dependency while I was pregnant was tough. I was a little cranky, and morning sickness made me an awful lot to deal with. Ever since I could stomach it again, I've been good at sticking to one cup in the morning. It still has to be rich and caffeinated. I'm nursing Owen, and don't want anything interrupting his nightly routine. We've finally gotten him on a schedule and settled in at night in the nursery at our new home. Sleep being of vital importance to us with an infant in the house, neither Trig nor I are jinxing it.

"I'm sure I've got some," Ghillie replies.

"I can get it." Aidy offers.

"No, sit down. It is your birthday." Her mother instructs. "Enjoy your company. Open your gifts."

Trig places his fork on his plate and takes Owen back to burp him. The baby spits up and, in true new dad style, Trig removes Owen's stocking cap using it to wipe the baby's face.

"He's only a few months old and you're already a pro," Don comments.

"I'm trying." Trig grins. He runs his fingers through our son's baby soft hair. Whispers of red have appeared over the past few weeks. My husband's face lights up watching Owen smile while fighting to keep his eyes open.

Aidy finishes opening the gift from Ghillie and Don. She picks up ours with the pink wrapping, organdy ribbon, and Sterling's sticker and shakes it. "I wonder what this could be?" She jests, tearing into the paper and lifting the lid of the box.

I worry my lip and Trig reaches for my hand under the table, lacing our fingers together.

"It's us." She's astonished. "Mom, look. It's all of us."

Aidy rushes to show Ghillie who brings the silver fame over for Don to take a peek at. He winks at me.

In the hospital, Don had wanted to take Aidy's picture with Owen and I. I think he's known all along I had none other than the one I won't give up. After years of declining, and pushing Don onto the other side of the camera, I asked the maternity ward nurse to take a snapshot. Not just of me and my son and daughter, but of all six of us.

Trig had two copies made. The match to this one sits on my dresser in an identical Sterling's frame. It's next to the one he'd given to me when we moved, and the picture he'd found of me holding my newborn daughter.

Thank you for reading Splinter of Hope! I hope you love Trig and Kimber as much as I do. If you got caught up in Trig and Kimber's angsty love story, you can get a second glimpse into their life in **Holding Onto Hope**.

Enjoy the following preview of the next book in the Shattered Hearts of Carolina series featuring Aidy and her first love, Morgan, in **Shred of Decency**…

————————

SHRED OF DECENCY

"You should report this, sweetheart." The nurse practitioner's voice is soothing, and in harsh contrast to the echo of the speculum clattering onto the metal tray. She rolls it out of the way, placing a reassuring hand on my shoulder as I sit up.

I don't want anyone touching me. Shrugging her off, I reach for my clothes heaped on a nearby chair. I pull my panties and slouchy sweatpants up to cover myself before a physician excuses themselves from the room during a normal exam.

"What is there to report?" I ask with a quiver in my low voice, hardly audible as the vents in the small room kick on.

My internal thermometer is off. I'm bone-chilled and my skin is prickly hot. Tunnels of darkness and spots have threatened my vision for hours. The walls have been closing in, even when I walked outside across campus to the health center.

I push up my sweatshirt sleeves and am as quick to drag them back down, covering my wrists. Having my skin exposed to the nurse was enough. I don't want anyone to see any part of me and will risk becoming overheated and passing out to keep covered.

After slipping on my shoes, I focus on my bent knees. She crumples the blue paper that covered the tray and the trash can clangs open and shut. Coming into the clinic was a mistake. I was trying to prove to myself I was being stupid. That if I didn't remember what happened then it couldn't possibly be the truth.

The nurse steps in front of me. She holds out an appointment card. I take it because my parents raised me to mind my manners and, in this situation, I don't know how else to act.

"Aidy, you may not have bruises on the outside, but it doesn't mean there aren't any on the inside. Your confusion is obvious." She looks at me with so much sympathy. It's as if she can see red gushing out of the gaping wound in my heart. "Sweetheart, there are people who can help you. I'd be glad to stay with you the whole time if you need someone. If it means anything, I don't think you changed your mind."

Gee, what made that obvious? I think to myself. I have zero inclination to be sarcastic when she's trying her best not to rattle me any more than I already am.

I'd confided I wasn't on birth control when we were reviewing my medical history. There was no reason for a healthy nineteen-year-old to be when they weren't sexually active. My periods were enviable; a few light days on the twenty-eighth of each month. Can I be any luckier? Even February has that number on the calendar. Because of this, I've never had an internal exam until a few minutes ago. I hadn't been sure what to expect, but the way the speculum hung from my lower area reinforced the discomfort I'd already been feeling.

"It's best to report a rape right away."

The shame and self-loathing connected to the word is too much for me. I haven't been able to meet her eyes the whole time. How did I allow myself to become a woman who had to deal with these emotions?

"I can see how troubled you are accepting this, Aidy. I want you to understand I'm here no matter what you decide." She wraps her hand around my fingers, now holding the appointment card. "Come back this week no matter what your choice is. I'd like to see for myself you're okay. Can you do that for me? It would make me feel better, and I'd be glad to answer any questions you think of between now and then."

I finally look up. The kindness in her face reminds me of my mom's. She wants to help me, but this isn't a skinned elbow from landing on the grass when I skidded, missing while trying to catch a fly ball. I want to forget whatever game this is because my name wasn't supposed to be on the roster. I'd gladly rewind to the point where I booked this appointment. I'd almost rather have lived the rest of my life in limbo than know this happened to me.

I stuff the card into my hoodie pocket next to the

wallet holding my Pinewood College ID. Clutching them as if a thief will steal them the way my virginity has been stolen, I run-walk back to my dorm.

I'm filled with anxiety and unanswerable questions. How could he have done this to me? How could I have been so naive? Was it even him? And if it wasn't, then *who*?

I take the stairs up to the fourth floor because I'm petrified to be with anyone in an enclosed space. Halfway up, I start to cry because maybe waiting for a group of people to get on the elevator was safer. I fall to my ass on the concrete step, choking down sobs. The rocky texture of the formed stone grinds into my bottom, making my butt hurt. I may not have bruises, but it hasn't stopped everything from aching. When I regain the strength to walk again, I make it to my door. With my head ducked low, I fumble with the lock. It opens and the door swings wide. In a swift motion, I have it shut and flip the bolt.

The wet towel I'd used to shower with has fallen on the floor and there is the faint outline of the puddle my shampoo caddy had sat in while it dried. The sight of my long twin bed attracts my attention. Its perfect hospital corners mock me. I couldn't stand the rumpled sheets, thinking about what's been done to me without my consent. I'd tidied up as best as possible in between trips to the bathroom to clean myself off, waiting for my lower GI to settle, and pressing cool compresses between my legs. I sat in my roommate's Papasan chair for twenty-four hours before the burning sensation from the angry hives on my inner thighs became too much to handle and I called the health center.

I approach my desk and take a puff from the inhaler for my asthma. The nurse said with my latex allergy it was best to keep using it the way I have been. I thought it was a simple anxiety attack that had made it difficult to breathe. The allergy is another way she saw through to what he's done to me. I am, *was* a smart girl. I would have told him we couldn't use those types of condoms.

I take the throw pillow off the chair and lie down on the area rug with my back away from the bed. My slouchy sweats are the only thing covering me. The appointment card pokes into my stomach.

My mind reels over all the questions the nurse asked that I was unable to answer, repeating the ones I could as if they can save me still. *How many partners have you had?* None. *Did you know you were allergic to latex?* Yes. *Do you remember anything?*

I remember getting ready and being excited to wear the new Rincon dress I'd found on a clearance rack because the weather going into fall has been so beautiful. The curved, athletic hem scooped above my knee, which I loved since I have longer legs and a shorter torso, and simple summer dresses are my jam since you can put them on and run out the door when you're late.

It's the beginning of my sophomore year. Students have just moved back to campus. My new roommate went home for the weekend. When we agreed to bunk together, I was aware she picked up as many hours as she could at her job. I don't go places alone at night, and my other girlfriends—many of whom scattered amongst other dorms and Greek houses this year— hadn't approached me with a plan. So, when Brandon invited me to a welcome back kegger on Friday night, I agreed.

I'd met him while standing in line at the college store for what seemed like an eternity. We'd struck up a conversation, which led to lunch together in the cafeteria a few times over the past week.

When we got to the party, I saw a friend I hadn't seen yet this semester. While she and I were catching up, he asked if I'd like a drink and took off to get our beverages. I didn't think anything of the grin on his face as he walked back with those two red plastic cups. He'd bought me a fountain drink not eight hours earlier. I'd let him put the plastic tops onto our cups and the straw in mine while I'd reached for some napkins to wipe up a spill.

Bass pounded from the speakers in the house and the music got incredibly loud, so we went outside to talk. The sounds became more muted and my recollections foggy. I have no clue how I got back to my room or if Brandon was the one who brought me here. I woke up on Saturday feeling like a truck hit me. My dress was rumpled past my midsection. The tie at the waist bound at my armpits. My bra was trapped underneath, unclasped in the back. The straps hung loose at my shoulders. I later found the underwear I'd worn in a knot where the sheet tucks into the mattress. The ache between my legs didn't register at first. My head throbbed too hard. Then all I thought, as searing pain stabbed inside me, burning my thighs, was how this couldn't have happened? I would've known.

I waited twenty years for that moment. It was supposed to be...Unforgettable.

There's no erasing the past few hours from my memory and back in my dorm, lying on my side, the seconds tick by like minutes. Time stands still, mocking me. I stare at the dust bunny clinging to the mini-fridge under my roommate, Hailey's, bed watching it get pushed around by the whirr of the motor as it clicks on and off. As if attached by a tiny invisible chain, the puff of dirt never lets go of its captor.

The sunlight has faded to a deep navy shadowing the room when a key tumbles in the lock. Hailey flips on the light, throwing her clean laundry bag and the backpack she took home with her on her mattress. Like mine, her parents live in the area and her weekend job at a cinema is near their house.

"What are you doing on the floor?" she asks in a

laughing tone, suggesting I've partied too much while she was away.

"I don't feel well. I think I came down with something." I'm surprised at how easy the lie rolls off my tongue.

"Make sure you go to health services tomorrow if it gets any worse," Hailey says, scooting a trash basket closer in case I'll need it in an emergency.

"I've already been."

I've had blood taken. Urine. Pictures. The nurse gave me the morning-after pill to be "on the safe side". Safe seems like a comical word. Safe is pouring your own drink. Safe is not having sex with someone who is blacked out so that they don't have to safely use medication to prevent an unwanted pregnancy. Should I be grateful whoever it was used a condom to be safe when it protected them?

"You want a blanket?" She tugs at my bedding.

"No!" I sit up too fast and have to lay right back down when my head spins. I cover my eyes with the crook of my elbow. The material of my sweatshirts absorbs the moisture from my eyes and hides the harsh and critical light shining down on me.

Ready to read more?
Shred of Decency is available now!
www.jodykaye.com/shredofdecency

____

I wish I could write as fast as you read. My brain sparked with the original concept for this series the first year I began publishing. It wound up getting back-burnered for so long I honestly never thought these books would get written.

During the fall of 2019, I'd also taken a serious step back to consider what I loved about indie publishing, what I didn't, what was working, and what wasn't. About to enter my 4th year (Holy Moly!), I understood two things:

The first is for me being indie means I'm in control. To a decent extent, that includes my stress level. Maintaining longevity means avoiding burn out. No matter how hard I wish it were different, I'm only capable of writing so many books in a year.

The second? I'm a series writer. I love backstory. I love the way character's personalities bounce off of one another as they grow from one book to the next. I love revisiting plot lines and hiding Easter Eggs in stories, whether or not the reader catches onto them.

It's not to say every book I pen will be part of a series, but I know my strengths lie in my passion. I pick apart books of every romance sub-genre written in a similar style to mine. As a reader, I live in those books. As a writer, I live *for* those books because they're invaluable at teaching me craft the best way I learn.

After establishing the Kingsbrier Quintuplets series and the Legacy spin-off, Shattered Hearts of Carolina should have been a no-brainer. However, I sat at my desk for weeks going over chapters I'd written years ago, not understanding who these people were, the world they lived in or how to create a universe for the initial book concepts. What I thought these books were going to be years ago didn't align with the books I'd published or match reader expectations.

And I stressed out!

The quints went from A to Z. The first Shattered Hearts book I was attempting to plot was somewhere around point KMN (kill me now, if you're not a Big Bang Theory rerun enthusiast.) The secondary characters—which if you're a long-time reader you know my secondary cast is never okay with taking a back seat to my main character's storylines—were lifeless. I didn't understand their motivations for anything. So, I set about reverse-engineering an entire universe.

My very first task was tearing a character in half who wasn't working. Trig started out as part of Skye, whom you'll meet in the next few books. Trig had a name, a job, and not much else. I didn't even know what he looked like. Trig didn't have a backstory, and inviting one more person to the party in my brain overwhelmed me. Unwilling to concede defeat, I popped into Quintessential, my reader group, and shamelessly asked them to construct their ideal book boyfriend.

I have never not created my own characters and giving my readership this power was a HUGE step for me. I wasn't even sure if they'd be interested.

Boy, was I wrong.

Up to the task, my Quinters had every detail of Trig nailed down in hours. A day later, I was jotting notes stream of consciousness and the need for a new female character/friendship popped into my head. Trig literally growled in my ear the way you've heard me comment that Brier does and I stopped because even used to writer-brain, when your characters start taking over your thoughts it's a little disconcerting!

It got me wondering, *what would happen if I gave the*

Quinters her name? Again, my readers rose to the challenge. In two days, I had two brand new characters to breathe life into. A week later, Splinter of Hope was a complete draft manuscript. From there, three more brand-new books evolved, forming the foundation at the mill.

I'm eternally grateful because this series never would have gotten from page to published without the help from my amazing readers!

Also by Jody Kaye

Shattered Hearts of Carolina
Splinter of Hope
Shred of Decency
Sliver of Truth
Holding Onto Hope
Home Wrecker
Deep Gap
Bleeding Heart
Shattered Soul

The Kingsbrier Legacy
Love Thy Neighbor
Gray Sin
Going Down

The Kingsbrier Quintuplets
Eric
Brier
Daveigh
Miss Cavanaugh
Cavanaugh
Adam
Colette
Colton

The Canvas Duet
Canvas
Imprint

To view more great titles, sign up for Jody Kaye's newsletter, or find her on social media go to www.jodykaye.com or

Scan Now!

About the Author

Jody's husband asked what she'd been doing all day. After five years she finally confessed, "When no one is around, I write."

Okay, it was more like a bunch of stammering and trying to get out of saying a thing. Jody's a writer. You want it pretty. Let's compromise.

"Just finish one," he said, challenging her to complete a story and share it. Little did he know that those words of encouragement meant they'd return from a family vacation with a wild and defiant set of quintuplets stumbling their way into adulthood. Wasn't raising their three sons enough?

A native of nowhere, Jody settled in New England for 17 years before agreeing to uproot her brood of boys and move to North Carolina. She's a part-time graphic designer and marketeer with over twenty years' experience, and full-time writer. If Jody ever gets lost, you'll find her reading, all the while hoping that her ravenous children haven't eaten all the ingredients before she's cooked dinner.

Add your voice and help readers discover
this love story by writing a review!